SARR

Honoré d

I was buried in one of those profound reveries to which everybody, even a frivolous man, is subject in the midst of the most uproarious festivities. The clock on the Elysee-Bourbon had just struck midnight. Seated in a window recess and concealed behind the undulating folds of a curtain of watered silk, I was able to contemplate at my leisure the garden of the mansion at which I was passing the evening. The trees, being partly covered with snow, were outlined indistinctly against the grayish background formed by a cloudy sky, barely whitened by the moon. Seen through the medium of that strange atmosphere, they bore a vague resemblance to spectres carelessly enveloped in their shrouds, a gigantic image of the famous *Dance of Death*. Then, turning in the other direction, I could gaze admiringly upon the dance of the living! a magnificent salon, with walls of silver and gold, with gleaming chandeliers, and bright with the light of many candles. There the loveliest, the wealthiest women in Paris, bearers of the proudest titles, moved hither and thither, fluttered from room to room in swarms, stately and gorgeous, dazzling with diamonds; flowers on their heads and breasts, in their hair, scattered over their dresses or lying in garlands at their feet. Light quiverings of the body, voluptuous movements, made the laces and gauzes and silks swirl about their graceful figures. Sparkling glances here and there eclipsed the lights and the blaze of the diamonds, and fanned the flame of hearts already burning too brightly. I detected also significant nods of the head for lovers and repellent attitudes for husbands. The exclamation of the card-players at every unexpected *coup*, the jingle of gold, mingled with music and the murmur of conversation; and to put the finishing touch to the vertigo of that multitude, intoxicated by all the seductions the world can offer, a perfume-laden atmosphere and general exaltation acted upon their over-wrought imaginations. Thus, at my right was the depressing, silent image of death; at my left the decorous bacchanalia of life; on the one side nature, cold and gloomy, and in mourning garb; on the other side, man on pleasure bent. And, standing on the borderland of those two incongruous pictures, which repeated thousands of times in diverse ways, make Paris the most entertaining and most philosophical city in the world, I played a mental *macedoine*[*], half jesting, half funereal. With my left foot I kept time to the music, and the other felt as if it were in a tomb. My leg was, in fact, frozen by one of those draughts which congeal one half of the body while the other suffers from the intense heat of the salons—a state of things not unusual at balls.

[*] *Macedoine*, in the sense in which it is here used, is a game, or rather a series of games, of cards, each player, when it is his turn to deal, selecting the game to be played.

"Monsieur de Lanty has not owned this house very long, has he?"

"Oh, yes! It is nearly ten years since the Marechal de Carigliano sold it to him."

"Ah!"

"These people must have an enormous fortune."

"They surely must."

"What a magnificent party! It is almost insolent in its splendor."

"Do you imagine they are as rich as Monsieur de Nucingen or Monsieur de Gondreville?"

"Why, don't you know?"

I leaned forward and recognized the two persons who were talking as members of that inquisitive genus which, in Paris, busies itself exclusively with the *Whys* and *Hows*. *Where does he come from? Who are they? What's the matter with him? What has she done?* They lowered their voices and walked away in order to talk more at their ease on some retired couch. Never was a more promising mine laid open to seekers after mysteries. No one knew from what country the Lanty family came, nor to what source—commerce, extortion, piracy, or inheritance—they owed a fortune estimated at several millions. All the members of the family spoke Italian, French, Spanish, English, and German, with sufficient fluency to lead one to suppose that they had lived long among those different peoples. Were they gypsies? were they buccaneers?

"Suppose they're the devil himself," said divers young politicians, "they entertain mighty well."

"The Comte de Lanty may have plundered some *Casbah* for all I care; I would like to marry his daughter!" cried a philosopher.

Who would not have married Marianina, a girl of sixteen, whose beauty realized the fabulous conceptions of Oriental poets! Like the Sultan's daughter in the tale of the *Wonderful Lamp*, she should have remained always veiled. Her singing obscured the imperfect talents of the Malibrans, the Sontags, and the Fodors, in whom some one dominant quality always mars the perfection of the whole; whereas Marianina combined in equal degree purity of tone, exquisite feeling, accuracy of time and intonation, science, soul, and delicacy. She was the type of that hidden poesy, the link which connects all the arts and which always eludes those who seek it. Modest, sweet, well-informed, and clever, none could eclipse Marianina unless it was her mother.

Have you ever met one of those women whose startling beauty defies the assaults of time, and who seem at thirty-six more desirable than they could have been fifteen years earlier? Their faces are impassioned souls; they fairly sparkle; each feature gleams with intelligence; each possesses a brilliancy of its own, especially in the light. Their captivating eyes attract or repel, speak or are silent; their gait is artlessly seductive; their voices unfold the melodious treasures of the most coquettishly sweet and tender tones. Praise of their beauty, based upon comparisons, flatters the most sensitive self-esteem. A movement of their eyebrows, the slightest play of the eye, the curling of the lip, instils a sort of terror in those whose lives and happiness depend upon their favor. A maiden inexperienced in love and easily moved by words may allow herself to be seduced; but in dealing with women of this sort, a man must be able, like M. de Jaucourt, to refrain from crying out when, in hiding him in a closet, the lady's maid crushes two of his fingers in the crack of a door. To love one of these omnipotent sirens is to stake one's life, is it not? And that, perhaps, is why we love them so passionately! Such was the Comtesse de Lanty.

Filippo, Marianina's brother, inherited, as did his sister, the Countess' marvelous beauty. To tell the whole story in a word, that young man was a living image of Antinous, with somewhat slighter proportions. But how well such a slender and delicate figure accords with youth, when an olive complexion, heavy eyebrows, and the gleam of a velvety eye promise virile passions, noble ideas for the future! If Filippo remained in the hearts of young women as a type of manly beauty, he likewise remained in the memory of all mothers as the best match in France.

The beauty, the great wealth, the intellectual qualities, of these two children came entirely from their mother. The Comte de Lanty was a short, thin, ugly little man, as dismal as a Spaniard, as great a bore as a banker. He was looked upon, however, as a profound politician, perhaps because he rarely laughed, and was always quoting M. de Metternich or Wellington.

This mysterious family had all the attractiveness of a poem by Lord Byron, whose difficult passages were translated differently by each person in fashionable society; a poem that grew more obscure and more sublime from strophe to strophe. The reserve which Monsieur and Madame de Lanty maintained concerning their origin, their past lives, and their relations with the four quarters of the globe would not, of itself, have been for long a subject of wonderment in Paris. In no other country, perhaps, is Vespasian's maxim more thoroughly understood. Here gold pieces, even when stained with blood or mud, betray nothing, and represent everything. Provided that good society knows the amount of your fortune, you are classed among those figures which equal yours, and no one asks to see your credentials, because everybody knows how little they cost. In a city where social problems are solved by algebraic equations, adventurers have many chances in their favor. Even if this family were of gypsy extraction, it was so wealthy, so attractive, that fashionable society could well afford to overlook its little mysteries. But, unfortunately, the enigmatical history of the Lanty family offered a perpetual subject of curiosity, not unlike that aroused by the novels of Anne Radcliffe.

People of an observing turn, of the sort who are bent upon finding out where you buy your candelabra, or who ask you what rent you pay when they are pleased with your apartments, had noticed, from time to time, the appearance of an extraordinary personage at the fetes, concerts, balls, and routs given by the countess. It was a man. The first time that he was seen in the house was at a concert, when he seemed to have been drawn to the salon by Marianina's enchanting voice.

"I have been cold for the last minute or two," said a lady near the door to her neighbor.

The stranger, who was standing near the speaker, moved away.

"This is very strange! now I am warm," she said, after his departure. "Perhaps you will call me mad, but I cannot help thinking that my neighbor, the gentleman in black who just walked away, was the cause of my feeling cold."

Ere long the exaggeration to which people in society are naturally inclined, produced a large and growing crop of the most amusing ideas, the most curious expressions, the most absurd fables concerning this mysterious individual. Without being precisely a vampire, a ghoul, a fictitious man, a sort of Faust or Robin des Bois, he partook of the nature of all these anthropomorphic conceptions, according to those persons who were addicted to the fantastic. Occasionally some German would take for realities these ingenious jests of Parisian evil-speaking. The stranger was simply *an old man*. Some young men, who were accustomed to decide the future of Europe every morning in a few fashionable phrases, chose to see in the stranger some great criminal, the possessor of enormous wealth. Novelists described the old man's life and gave some really interesting details of the atrocities committed by him while he was in the service of the Prince of Mysore. Bankers, men of a more positive nature, devised a specious fable.

"Bah!" they would say, shrugging their broad shoulders pityingly, "that little old fellow's a *Genoese head!*"

"If it is not an impertinent question, monsieur, would you have the kindness to tell me what you mean by a Genoese head?"

"I mean, monsieur, that he is a man upon whose life enormous sums depend, and whose good health is undoubtedly essential to the continuance of this family's income. I remember that I once heard a mesmerist, at Madame d'Espard's, undertake to prove by very specious historical deductions, that this old man, if put under the magnifying glass, would turn out to be the famous Balsamo, otherwise called Cagliostro. According to this modern alchemist, the Sicilian had escaped death, and amused himself making gold for his grandchildren. And the Bailli of Ferette declared that he recognized in this extraordinary personage the Comte de Saint-Germain."

Such nonsense as this, put forth with the assumption of superior cleverness, with the air of raillery, which in our day characterize a society devoid of faith, kept alive vague suspicions concerning the Lanty family. At last, by a strange combination of circumstances, the members of that family justified the conjectures of society by adopting a decidedly mysterious course of conduct with this old man, whose life was, in a certain sense, kept hidden from all investigations.

If he crossed the threshold of the apartment he was supposed to occupy in the Lanty mansion, his appearance always caused a great sensation in the family. One would have supposed that it was an event of the greatest importance. Only Filippo, Marianina, Madame de Lanty, and an old servant enjoyed the privilege of assisting the unknown to walk, to rise, to sit down. Each one of them kept a close watch on his slightest movements. It seemed as if he were some enchanted person upon whom the happiness, the life, or the fortune of all depended. Was it fear or affection? Society could discover no indication which enabled them to solve this problem. Concealed for months at a time in the depths of an unknown sanctuary, this familiar spirit suddenly emerged, furtively as it were, unexpectedly, and appeared in the salons like the fairies of old, who alighted from their winged dragons to disturb festivities to which they had not been invited. Only the most experienced observers could divine the anxiety, at such times, of the masters of the house, who were peculiarly skilful in concealing their feelings. But sometimes, while dancing a quadrille, the too ingenuous Marianina would cast a terrified glance at the old man, whom she watched closely from the circle of dancers. Or perhaps Filippo would leave his place and glide through the crowd to where he stood, and remain beside him, affectionate and watchful, as if the touch of man, or the faintest breath, would shatter that extraordinary creature. The countess would try to draw nearer to him without apparently intending to join him; then, assuming a manner and an expression in which servility and affection, submissiveness and tyranny, were equally noticeable, she would say two or three words, to which the old man almost always deferred; and he would disappear, led, or I might better say carried away, by her. If Madame de Lanty were not present, the Count would employ a thousand ruses to reach his side; but it always seemed as if he found difficulty in inducing him to listen, and he treated him like a spoiled child, whose mother gratifies his whims and at the same time suspects mutiny. Some prying persons having ventured to question the Comte de Lanty indiscreetly, that cold and reserved individual seemed not to understand their questions. And so, after many attempts, which the circumspection of all the members of the family rendered fruitless, no one sought to discover a secret so well guarded. Society spies, triflers, and politicians, weary of the strife, ended by ceasing to concern themselves about the mystery.

But at that moment, it may be, there were in those gorgeous salons philosophers who said to themselves, as they discussed an ice or a sherbet, or placed their empty punch glasses on a tray:

"I should not be surprised to learn that these people are knaves. That old fellow who keeps out of sight and appears only at the equinoxes or solstices, looks to me exactly like an assassin."

"Or a bankrupt."

"There's very little difference. To destroy a man's fortune is worse than to kill the man himself."

"I bet twenty louis, monsieur; there are forty due me."

"Faith, monsieur; there are only thirty left on the cloth."

"Just see what a mixed company there is! One can't play cards in peace."

"Very true. But it's almost six months since we saw the Spirit. Do you think he's a living being?"

"Well, barely."

These last remarks were made in my neighborhood by persons whom I did not know, and who passed out of hearing just as I was summarizing in one last thought my reflections, in which black and white, life and death, were inextricably mingled. My wandering imagination, like my eyes, contemplated alternately the festivities, which had now reached the climax of their splendor, and the gloomy picture presented by the gardens. I have no idea how long I meditated upon those two faces of the human medal; but I was suddenly aroused by the stifled laughter of a young woman. I was stupefied at the picture presented to my eyes. By virtue of one of the strangest of nature's freaks, the thought half draped in black, which was tossing about in my brain, emerged from it and stood before me personified, living; it had come forth like Minerva from Jupiter's brain, tall and strong; it was at once a hundred years old and twenty-two; it was alive and dead. Escaped from his chamber, like a madman from his cell, the little old man had evidently crept behind a long line of people who were listening attentively to Marianina's voice as she finished the cavatina from *Tancred.* He seemed to have come up through the floor, impelled by some stage mechanism. He stood for a moment motionless and sombre, watching the festivities, a murmur of which had perhaps reached his ears. His almost somnambulistic preoccupation was so concentrated upon things that, although he was in the midst of many people, he saw nobody. He had taken his place unceremoniously beside one of the most fascinating women in Paris, a young and graceful dancer, with slender figure, a face as fresh as a child's, all pink and white, and so fragile, so transparent, that it seemed that a man's glance must pass through her as the sun's rays pass through flawless glass. They stood there before me, side by side, so close together, that the stranger rubbed against the gauze dress, and the wreaths of flowers, and the hair, slightly crimped, and the floating ends of the sash.

I had brought that young woman to Madame de Lanty's ball. As it was her first visit to that house, I forgave her her stifled laugh; but I hastily made an imperious sign which abashed her and inspired respect for her neighbor. She sat down beside me. The old man did not choose to leave the charming creature, to whom he clung capriciously with the silent and apparently causeless obstinacy to which very old persons are subject, and which makes them resemble children. In order to sit down beside the young lady he needed a folding-chair. His slightest movements were marked by the inert heaviness, the stupid hesitancy,

7

which characterize the movements of a paralytic. He sat slowly down upon his chair with great caution, mumbling some unintelligible words. His cracked voice resembled the noise made by a stone falling into a well. The young woman nervously pressed my hand, as if she were trying to avoid a precipice, and shivered when that man, at whom she happened to be looking, turned upon her two lifeless, sea-green eyes, which could be compared to nothing save tarnished mother-of-pearl.

"I am afraid," she said, putting her lips to my ear.

"You can speak," I replied; "he hears with great difficulty."

"You know him, then?"

"Yes."

Thereupon she summoned courage to scrutinize for a moment that creature for which no human language has a name, form without substance, a being without life, or life without action. She was under the spell of that timid curiosity which impels women to seek perilous excitement, to gaze at chained tigers and boa-constrictors, shuddering all the while because the barriers between them are so weak. Although the little old man's back was bent like a day-laborer's, it was easy to see that he must formerly have been of medium height. His excessive thinness, the slenderness of his limbs, proved that he had always been of slight build. He wore black silk breeches which hung about his fleshless thighs in folds, like a lowered veil. An anatomist would instinctively have recognized the symptoms of consumption in its advanced stages, at sight of the tiny legs which served to support that strange frame. You would have said that they were a pair of cross-bones on a gravestone. A feeling of profound horror seized the heart when a close scrutiny revealed the marks made by decrepitude upon that frail machine.

He wore a white waistcoat embroidered with gold, in the old style, and his linen was of dazzling whiteness. A shirt-frill of English lace, yellow with age, the magnificence of which a queen might have envied, formed a series of yellow ruffles on his breast; but upon him the lace seemed rather a worthless rag than an ornament. In the centre of the frill a diamond of inestimable value gleamed like a sun. That superannuated splendor, that display of treasure, of great intrinsic worth, but utterly without taste, served to bring out in still bolder relief the strange creature's face. The frame was worthy of the portrait. That dark face was full of angles and furrowed deep in every direction; the chin was furrowed; there were great hollows at the temples; the eyes were sunken in yellow orbits. The maxillary bones, which his indescribable gauntness caused to protrude, formed deep cavities in the centre of both cheeks. These protuberances, as the light fell upon them, caused curious effects of light and shadow which deprived that face of its last vestige of resemblance to the human countenance. And then, too, the lapse of years had drawn the fine, yellow skin so close to the bones that it described a multitude of wrinkles everywhere, either circular like the ripples in the water caused by a stone which a child throws in, or star-shaped like a pane of glass cracked by a blow; but everywhere very deep, and as close together as the leaves of a closed book. We often see more hideous old men; but what contributed more than aught else to give to the spectre that rose before us the aspect of an artificial creation was the red and white paint with which he glistened. The eyebrows shone in the light with a lustre which disclosed a very well executed bit of painting. Luckily for the eye, saddened by such a mass of ruins, his corpse-like skull was concealed beneath a light wig, with innumerable curls which indicated extraordinary pretensions to elegance. Indeed, the feminine coquettishness of this fantastic apparition was emphatically asserted by the gold ear-rings which hung at his ears, by the rings containing stones of marvelous beauty which sparkled on his fingers, like the brilliants in a river of gems around a woman's neck. Lastly, this species of Japanese idol had constantly upon his blue lips, a fixed, unchanging smile, the shadow of an implacable and sneering laugh, like that of a death's head. As silent and motionless as a statue, he exhaled the musk-like odor of the old dresses which a duchess' heirs exhume from her wardrobe during the inventory. If the old man turned his eyes toward the company, it seemed that the movements of those globes, no longer capable of reflecting a gleam, were accomplished by an almost imperceptible effort; and, when the eyes stopped, he who was watching them was not certain finally that they had moved at all. As I saw, beside that human ruin, a young woman whose bare neck and arms and breast were white as snow; whose figure was well-rounded and beautiful in its youthful grace; whose hair, charmingly arranged above an alabaster forehead, inspired love; whose eyes did not receive but gave forth light, who was sweet and fresh, and whose fluffy curls, whose fragrant breath, seemed too heavy, too harsh, too overpowering for that shadow, for that man of dust—ah! the thought that came into my mind was of death and life, an imaginary arabesque, a half-hideous chimera, divinely feminine from the waist up.

"And yet such marriages are often made in society!" I said to myself.

"He smells of the cemetery!" cried the terrified young woman, grasping my arm as if to make sure of my protection, and moving about in a restless, excited way, which convinced me that she was very much frightened. "It's a horrible vision," she continued; "I cannot stay here any longer. If I look at him again I shall believe that Death himself has come in search of me. But is he alive?"

She placed her hand on the phenomenon, with the boldness which women derive from the violence of their wishes, but a cold sweat burst from her pores, for, the instant she touched the old man, she heard a cry like the noise made by a rattle. That shrill voice, if indeed it were a voice, escaped from a throat almost entirely dry. It was at once succeeded by a convulsive little cough like a child's, of a peculiar resonance. At that sound, Marianina, Filippo, and Madame de Lanty looked toward us, and their glances were like lightning flashes. The young woman wished that she were at the bottom of the Seine. She took my arm and pulled me away toward a boudoir. Everybody, men and women, made room for us to pass. Having reached the further end of the suite of reception-rooms, we entered a small semi-circular cabinet. My companion threw herself on a divan, breathing fast with terror, not knowing where she was.

"You are mad, madame," I said to her.

"But," she rejoined, after a moment's silence, during which I gazed at her in admiration, "is it my fault? Why does Madame de Lanty allow ghosts to wander round her house?"

"Nonsense," I replied; "you are doing just what fools do. You mistake a little old man for a spectre."

"Hush," she retorted, with the imposing, yet mocking, air which all women are so well able to assume when they are determined to put themselves in the right. "Oh! what a sweet boudoir!" she cried, looking about her. "Blue satin hangings always produce an admirable effect. How cool it is! Ah! the lovely picture!" she added, rising and standing in front of a magnificently framed painting.

We stood for a moment gazing at that marvel of art, which seemed the work of some supernatural brush. The picture represented Adonis stretched out on a lion's skin. The lamp, in an alabaster vase, hanging in the centre of the boudoir, cast upon the canvas a soft light which enabled us to grasp all the beauties of the picture.

"Does such a perfect creature exist?" she asked me, after examining attentively, and not without a sweet smile of satisfaction, the exquisite grace of the outlines, the attitude, the color, the hair, in fact everything.

"He is too beautiful for a man," she added, after such a scrutiny as she would have bestowed upon a rival.

Ah! how sharply I felt at that moment those pangs of jealousy in which a poet had tried in vain to make me believe! the jealousy of engravings, of pictures, of statues, wherein artists exaggerate human beauty, as a result of the doctrine which leads them to idealize everything.

"It is a portrait," I replied. "It is a product of Vien's genius. But that great painter never saw the original, and your admiration will be modified somewhat perhaps, when I tell you that this study was made from a statue of a woman."

"But who is it?"

I hesitated.

"I insist upon knowing," she added earnestly.

"I believe," I said, "that this *Adonis* represents a—a relative of Madame de Lanty."

I had the chagrin of seeing that she was lost in contemplation of that figure. She sat down in silence, and I seated myself beside her and took her hand without her noticing it. Forgotten for a portrait! At that moment we heard in the silence a woman's footstep and the faint rustling of a dress. We saw the youthful Marianina enter the boudoir, even more resplendent by reason of her grace and her fresh costume; she was walking slowly and leading with motherly care, with a daughter's solicitude, the spectre in human attire, who had driven us from the music-room; as she led him, she watched with some anxiety the slow movement of his feeble feet. They walked painfully across the boudoir to a door hidden in the hangings. Marianina knocked softly. Instantly a tall, thin man, a sort of familiar spirit, appeared as if by magic. Before entrusting the old man to this mysterious guardian, the lovely child, with deep veneration, kissed the ambulatory corpse, and her chaste caress was not without a touch of that graceful playfulness, the secret of which only a few privileged women possess.

"*Addio, addio!*" she said, with the sweetest inflection of her young voice.

She added to the last syllable a wonderfully executed trill, in a very low tone, as if to depict the overflowing affection of her heart by a poetic expression. The old man, suddenly arrested by some memory, remained on the threshold of that secret retreat. In the profound silence we heard the sigh that came forth form his breast; he removed the most beautiful of the rings with which his skeleton fingers were laden, and placed it in Marianina's bosom. The young madcap laughed, plucked out the ring, slipped it on one of her fingers over her glove, and ran hastily back toward the salon, where the orchestra were, at that moment, beginning the prelude of a contra-dance.

She spied us.

"Ah! were you here?" she said, blushing.

After a searching glance at us as if to question us, she ran away to her partner with the careless petulance of her years.

"What does this mean?" queried my young partner. "Is he her husband? I believe I am dreaming. Where am I?"

"You!" I retorted, "you, madame, who are easily excited, and who, understanding so well the most imperceptible emotions, are able to cultivate in a man's heart the most delicate of sentiments, without crushing it, without shattering it at the very outset, you who have compassion for the tortures of the heart, and who, with the wit of the Parisian, combine a passionate temperament worthy of Spain or Italy—"

11

She realized that my words were heavily charged with bitter irony; and, thereupon, without seeming to notice it, she interrupted me to say:

"Oh! you describe me to suit your own taste. A strange kind of tyranny! You wish me not to be *myself!*"

"Oh! I wish nothing," I cried, alarmed by the severity of her manner. "At all events, it is true, is it not, that you like to hear stories of the fierce passions, kindled in our heart by the enchanting women of the South?"

"Yes. And then?"

"Why, I will come to your house about nine o'clock to-morrow evening, and elucidate this mystery for you."

"No," she replied, with a pout; "I wish it done now."

"You have not yet given me the right to obey you when you say, 'I wish it.'"

"At this moment," she said, with an exhibition of coquetry of the sort that drives men to despair, "I have a most violent desire to know this secret. To-morrow it may be that I will not listen to you."

She smiled and we parted, she still as proud and as cruel, I as ridiculous, as ever. She had the audacity to waltz with a young aide-de-camp, and I was by turns angry, sulky, admiring, loving, and jealous.

"Until to-morrow," she said to me, as she left the ball about two o'clock in the morning.

"I won't go," I thought. "I give up. You are a thousand times more capricious, more fanciful, than—my imagination."

The next evening we were seated in front of a bright fire in a dainty little salon, she on a couch, I on cushions almost at her feet, looking up into her face. The street was silent. The lamp shed a soft light. It was one of those evenings which delight the soul, one of those moments which are never forgotten, one of those hours passed in peace and longing, whose charm is always in later years a source of regret, even when we are happier. What can efface the deep imprint of the first solicitations of love?

"Go on," she said. "I am listening."

"But I dare not begin. There are passages in the story which are dangerous to the narrator. If I become excited, you will make me hold my peace."

"Speak."

"I obey.

"Ernest-Jean Sarrasine was the only son of a prosecuting attorney of Franche-Comte," I began after a pause. "His father had, by faithful work, amassed a fortune which yielded an income of six to eight thousand francs, then considered a colossal fortune for an attorney in the provinces. Old Maitre Sarrasine, having but one child, determined to give him a thorough education; he hoped to make a magistrate of him, and to live long enough to see, in his old age, the grandson of Mathieu Sarrasine, a ploughman in the Saint-Die country, seated on the lilies, and dozing through the sessions for the greater glory of the Parliament; but Heaven had not that joy in store for the attorney. Young Sarrasine, entrusted to the care of the Jesuits at an early age, gave indications of an extraordinarily unruly disposition. His was the childhood of a man of talent. He would not study except as his inclination led him, often rebelled, and sometimes remained for whole hours at a time buried in tangled meditations, engaged now in watching his comrades at play, now in forming mental pictures of Homer's heroes. And, when he did choose to amuse himself, he displayed extraordinary ardor in his games. Whenever there was a contest of any sort between a comrade and himself, it rarely ended without bloodshed. If he were the weaker, he would use his teeth. Active and passive by turns, either lacking in aptitude, or too intelligent, his abnormal temperament caused him to distrust his masters as much as his schoolmates. Instead of learning the elements of the Greek language, he drew a picture of the reverend father who was interpreting a passage of Thucydides, sketched the teacher of mathematics, the prefect, the assistants, the man who administered punishment, and smeared all the walls with shapeless figures. Instead of singing the praises of the Lord in the chapel, he amused himself, during the services, by notching a bench; or, when he had stolen a piece of wood, he would carve the figure of some saint. If he had no wood or stone or pencil, he worked out his ideas with bread. Whether he copied the figures in the pictures which adorned the choir, or improvised, he always left at this seat rough sketches, whose obscene character drove the young fathers to despair; and the evil-tongued alleged that the Jesuits smiled at them. At last, if we are to believe college traditions, he was expelled because, while awaiting his turn to go to the confessional one Good Friday, he carved a figure of the Christ from a stick of wood. The impiety evidenced by that figure was too flagrant not to draw down chastisement on the artist. He had actually had the hardihood to place that decidedly cynical image on the top of the tabernacle!

"Sarrasine came to Paris to seek a refuge against the threats of a father's malediction. Having one of those strong wills which know no obstacles, he obeyed the behests of his genius and entered Bouchardon's studio. He worked all day and went about at night begging for subsistence. Bouchardon, marveling at the young artist's intelligence and rapid progress, soon divined his pupil's destitute condition; he assisted him, became attached to him, and treated him like his own child. Then, when Sarrasine's genius stood revealed in one of those works wherein future talent contends with the effervescence of youth, the generous Bouchardon tried to restore him to the old attorney's good graces.

The paternal wrath subsided in face of the famous sculptor's authority. All Besancon congratulated itself on having brought forth a future great man. In the first outburst of delight due to his flattered vanity, the miserly attorney supplied his son with the means to appear to advantage in society. The long and laborious study demanded by the sculptor's profession subdued for a long time Sarrasine's impetuous temperament and unruly genius. Bouchardon, foreseeing how violently the passions would some day rage in that youthful heart, as highly tempered perhaps as Michelangelo's, smothered its vehemence with constant toil. He succeeded in restraining within reasonable bounds Sarrasine's extraordinary impetuosity, by forbidding him to work, by proposing diversions when he saw that he was on the point of plunging into dissipation. But with that passionate nature, gentleness was always the most powerful of all weapons, and the master did not acquire great influence over his pupil until he had aroused his gratitude by fatherly kindness.

"At the age of twenty-two Sarrasine was forcibly removed from the salutary influence which Bouchardon exercised over his morals and his habits. He paid the penalty of his genius by winning the prize for sculpture founded by the Marquis de Marigny, Madame de Pompadour's brother, who did so much for art. Diderot praised Bouchardon's pupil's statue as a masterpiece. Not without profound sorrow did the king's sculptor witness the departure for Italy of a young man whose profound ignorance of the things of life he had, as a matter of principle, refrained from enlightening. Sarrasine was Bouchardon's guest for six years. Fanatically devoted to his art, as Canova was at a later day, he rose at dawn and went to the studio, there to remain until night, and lived with his muse alone. If he went to the Comedie-Francaise, he was dragged thither by his master. He was so bored at Madame Geoffrin's, and in the fashionable society to which Bouchardon tried to introduce him, that he preferred to remain alone, and held aloof from the pleasures of that licentious age. He had no other mistresses than sculpture and Clotilde, one of the celebrities of the Opera. Even that intrigue was of brief duration. Sarrasine was decidedly ugly, always badly dressed, and naturally so independent, so irregular in his private life, that the illustrious nymph, dreading some catastrophe, soon remitted the sculptor to love of the arts. Sophie Arnould made some witty remark on the subject. She was surprised, I think, that her colleague was able to triumph over statues.

"Sarrasine started for Italy in 1758. On the journey his ardent imagination took fire beneath a sky of copper and at the sight of the marvelous monuments with which the fatherland of the arts is strewn. He admired the statues, the frescoes, the pictures; and, fired with a spirit of emulation, he went on to Rome, burning to inscribe his name between the names of Michelangelo and Bouchardon. At first, therefore, he divided his time between his studio work and examination of the works of art which abound in Rome. He had already passed a fortnight in the ecstatic state into which all youthful imaginations fall at the sight of the queen of ruins, when he happened one evening to enter the Argentina theatre, in front of which there was an enormous crowd. He inquired the reasons for the presence of so great a throng, and every one answered by two names:

"'Zambinella! Jomelli!'

"He entered and took a seat in the pit, crowded between two unconscionably stout *abbati*, but luckily he was quite near the stage. The curtain rose. For the first time in his life he heard the music whose charms Monsieur Jean-Jacques Rousseau had extolled so eloquently at one of Baron d'Holbach's evening parties. The young sculptor's senses were lubricated, so to speak, by Jomelli's harmonious strains. The languorous peculiarities of those skilfully blended Italian voices plunged him in an ecstasy of delight. He sat there, mute and motionless, not even conscious of the crowding of the two priests. His soul poured out through his ears and his eyes. He seemed to be listening with every one of his pores. Suddenly a whirlwind of applause greeted the appearance of the prima donna. She came forward coquettishly to the footlights and curtsied to the audience with infinite grace. The brilliant light, the enthusiasm of a vast multitude, the illusion of the stage, the glamour of a costume which was most attractive for the time, all conspired in that woman's favor. Sarrasine cried aloud with pleasure. He saw before him at that moment the ideal beauty whose perfections he had hitherto sought here and there in nature, taking from one model, often of humble rank, the rounded outline of a shapely leg, from another the contour of the breast; from another her white shoulders; stealing the neck of that young girl, the hands of this woman, and the polished knees of yonder child, but never able to find beneath the cold skies of Paris the rich and satisfying creations of ancient Greece. La Zambinella displayed in her single person, intensely alive and delicate beyond words, all those exquisite proportions of the female form which he had so ardently longed to behold, and of which a sculptor is the most severe and at the same time the most passionate judge. She had an expressive mouth, eyes instinct with love, flesh of dazzling whiteness. And add to these details, which would have filled a painter's soul with rapture, all the marvelous charms of the Venuses worshiped and copied by the chisel of the Greeks. The artist did not tire of admiring the inimitable grace with which the arms were attached to the body, the wonderful roundness of the throat, the graceful curves described by the eyebrows and the nose, and the perfect oval of the face, the purity of its clean-cut lines, and the effect of the thick, drooping lashes which bordered the large and voluptuous eyelids. She was more than a woman; she was a masterpiece! In that unhoped-for creation there was love enough to enrapture all mankind, and beauties calculated to satisfy the most exacting critic.

"Sarrasine devoured with his eyes what seemed to him Pygmalion's statue descended from its pedestal. When La Zambinella sang, he was beside himself. He was cold; then suddenly he felt a fire burning in the secret depths of his being, in what, for lack of a better word, we call the heart. He did not applaud, he said nothing; he felt a mad impulse, a sort of frenzy of the sort that seizes us only at the age when there is a something indefinably terrible and infernal in our desires. Sarrasine longed to rush upon the stage and seize that woman. His strength, increased a hundredfold by a moral depression impossible to describe,—for such phenomena take place in a sphere inaccessible to human observation,—insisted upon manifesting itself with deplorable violence. Looking at him,

15

you would have said that he was a cold, dull man. Renown, science, future, life, prizes, all vanished.

"'To win her love or die!' Such was the sentence Sarrasine pronounced upon himself.

"He was so completely intoxicated that he no longer saw theatre, audience, or actors, no longer heard the music. Nay, more, there was no space between him and La Zambinella; he possessed her; his eyes, fixed steadfastly upon her, took possession of her. An almost diabolical power enabled him to feel the breath of that voice, to inhale the fragrant powder with which her hair was covered, to see the slightest inequalities of her face, to count the blue veins which threaded their way beneath the satiny skin. And that fresh, brisk voice of silvery *timbre*, flexible as a thread to which the faintest breath of air gives form, which it rolls and unrolls, tangles and blows away, that voice attacked his heart so fiercely that he more than once uttered an involuntary exclamation, extorted by the convulsive ecstasy too rarely evoked by human passions. He was soon obliged to leave the theatre. His trembling legs almost refused to bear him. He was prostrated, weak, like a nervous man who has given way to a terrible burst of anger. He had had such exquisite pleasure, or perhaps had suffered so, that his life had flowed away like water from an overturned vessel. He felt a void within him, a sense of goneness like the utter lack of strength which discourages a convalescent just recovering from a serious sickness. Overwhelmed by inexplicable melancholy, he sat down on the steps of a church. There, with his back resting against a pillar, he lost himself in a fit of meditation as confused as a dream. Passion had dealt him a crushing blow. On his return to his apartments he was seized by one of those paroxysms of activity which reveal to us the presence of new principles in our existence. A prey to that first fever of love which resembles pain as much as pleasure, he sought to defeat his impatience and his frenzy by sketching La Zambinella from memory. It was a sort of material meditation. Upon one leaf La Zambinella appeared in that pose, apparently calm and cold, affected by Raphael, Georgione, and all the great painters. On another, she was coyly turning her head as she finished a roulade, and seemed to be listening to herself. Sarrasine drew his mistress in all poses: he drew her unveiled, seated, standing, reclining, chaste, and amorous—interpreting, thanks to the delirious activity of his pencil, all the fanciful ideas which beset our imagination when our thoughts are completely engrossed by a mistress. But his frantic thoughts outran his pencil. He met La Zambinella, spoke to her, entreated her, exhausted a thousand years of life and happiness with her, placing her in all imaginable situations, trying the future with her, so to speak. The next day he sent his servant to hire a box near the stage for the whole season. Then, like all young men of powerful feelings, he exaggerated the difficulties of his undertaking, and gave his passion, for its first pasturage, the joy of being able to admire his mistress without obstacle. The golden age of love, during which we enjoy our own sentiments, and in which we are almost as happy by ourselves, was not likely to last long with Sarrasine. However, events surprised him when he was still under the spell of that springtime hallucination, as naive as it was voluptuous. In a week he lived a whole lifetime, occupied through the day in molding the clay with which he succeeded in copying

16

La Zambinella, notwithstanding the veils, the skirts, the waists, and the bows of ribbon which concealed her from him. In the evening, installed at an early hour in his box, alone, reclining on a sofa, he made for himself, like a Turk drunk with opium, a happiness as fruitful, as lavish, as he wished. First of all, he familiarized himself gradually with the too intense emotions which his mistress' singing caused him; then he taught his eyes to look at her, and was finally able to contemplate her at his leisure without fearing an explosion of concealed frenzy, like that which had seized him the first day. His passion became more profound as it became more tranquil. But the unsociable sculptor would not allow his solitude, peopled as it was with images, adorned with the fanciful creations of hope, and full of happiness, to be disturbed by his comrades. His love was so intense and so ingenuous, that he had to undergo the innocent scruples with which we are assailed when we love for the first time. As he began to realize that he would soon be required to bestir himself, to intrigue, to ask where La Zambinella lived, to ascertain whether she had a mother, an uncle, a guardian, a family,—in a word, as he reflected upon the methods of seeing her, of speaking to her, he felt that his heart was so swollen with such ambitious ideas, that he postponed those cares until the following day, as happy in his physical sufferings as in his intellectual pleasures."

"But," said Madame de Rochefide, interrupting me, "I see nothing of Marianina or her little old man in all this."

"You see nothing but him!" I cried, as vexed as an author for whom some one has spoiled the effect of a *coup de theatre*.

"For some days," I resumed after a pause, "Sarrasine had been so faithful in attendance in his box, and his glances expressed such passionate love, that his passion for La Zambinella's voice would have been the town-talk of Paris, if the episode had happened here; but in Italy, madame, every one goes to the theatre for his own enjoyment, with all his own passions, with a heartfelt interest which precludes all thought of espionage with opera-glasses. However, the sculptor's frantic admiration could not long escape the notice of the performers, male and female. One evening the Frenchman noticed that they were laughing at him in the wings. It is hard to say what violent measures he might have resorted to, had not La Zambinella come on the stage. She cast at Sarrasine one of those eloquent glances which often say more than women intend. That glance was a complete revelation in itself. Sarrasine was beloved!

"'If it is a mere caprice,' he thought, already accusing his mistress of too great ardor, 'she does not know the sort of domination to which she is about to become subject. Her caprice will last, I trust, as long as my life.'

"At that moment, three light taps on the door of his box attracted the artist's attention. He opened the door. An old woman entered with an air of mystery.

"'Young man,' she said, 'if you wish to be happy, be prudent. Wrap yourself in a cloak, pull a broad-brimmed hat over your eyes, and be on the Rue du Corso, in front of the Hotel d'Espagne, about ten o'clock to-night.'

"'I will be there,' he replied, putting two louis in the duenna's wrinkled hand.

"He rushed from his box, after a sign of intelligence to La Zambinella, who lowered her voluptuous eyelids modestly, like a woman overjoyed to be understood at last. Then he hurried home, in order to borrow from his wardrobe all the charms it could loan him. As he left the theatre, a stranger grasped his arm.

"'Beware, Signor Frenchman,' he said in his ear. 'This is a matter of life and death. Cardinal Cicognara is her protector, and he is no trifler.'

"If a demon had placed the deep pit of hell between Sarrasine and La Zambinella, he would have crossed it with one stride at that moment. Like the horses of the immortal gods described by Homer, the sculptor's love had traversed vast spaces in a twinkling.

"'If death awaited me on leaving the house, I would go the more quickly,' he replied.

"'*Poverino!* cried the stranger, as he disappeared.

"To talk of danger to a man in love is to sell him pleasure. Sarrasine's valet had never seen his master so painstaking in the matter of dress. His finest sword, a gift from Bouchardon, the bow-knot Clotilde gave him, his coat with gold braid, his waistcoat of cloth of silver, his gold snuff-box, his valuable watch, everything was taken from its place, and he arrayed himself like a maiden about to appear before her first lover. At the appointed hour, drunk with love and boiling over with hope, Sarrasine, his nose buried in his cloak, hurried to the rendezvous appointed by the old woman. She was waiting.

"'You are very late,' she said. 'Come.'

"She led the Frenchman through several narrow streets and stopped in front of a palace of attractive appearance. She knocked; the door opened. She led Sarrasine through a labyrinth of stairways, galleries, and apartments which were lighted only by uncertain gleams of moonlight, and soon reached a door through the cracks of which stole a bright light, and from which came the joyous sound of several voices. Sarrasine was suddenly blinded when, at a word from the old woman, he was admitted to that mysterious apartment and found himself in a salon as brilliantly lighted as it was sumptuously furnished; in the centre stood a bountifully supplied table, laden with inviolable bottles, with laughing decanters whose red facets sparkled merrily. He recognized the singers from the theatre, male and female, mingled with charming women, all ready to begin an artists' spree and waiting only for him. Sarrasine restrained a feeling of displeasure and put a good face on the matter. He had hoped for a dimly lighted chamber, his mistress leaning over a brazier, a jealous rival within two steps, death and love, confidences exchanged in low tones, heart to heart, hazardous kisses, and faces so near together that La Zambinella's hair would have touched caressingly his desire-laden brow, burning with happiness.

"'*Vive la folie!* he cried. '*Signori e belle donne*, you will allow me to postpone my revenge and bear witness to my gratitude for the welcome you offer a poor sculptor.'

"After receiving congratulations not lacking in warmth from most of those present, whom he knew by sight, he tried to approach the couch on which La Zambinella was nonchalantly reclining. Ah! how his heart beat when he spied a tiny foot in one of those slippers which—if you will allow me to say so, madame—formerly imparted to a woman's feet such a coquettish, voluptuous look that I cannot conceive how men could resist them. Tightly fitting white stockings with green clocks, short skirts, and the pointed, high-heeled slippers of Louis XV.'s time contributed somewhat, I fancy, to the demoralization of Europe and the clergy."

"Somewhat!" exclaimed the marchioness. "Have you read nothing, pray?"

"La Zambinella," I continued, smiling, "had boldly crossed her legs, and as she prattled swung the upper one, a duchess' attitude very well suited to her capricious type of beauty, overflowing with a certain attractive suppleness. She had laid aside her stage costume, and wore a waist which outlined a slender figure, displayed to the best advantage by a *panier* and a satin dress embroidered with blue flowers. Her breast, whose treasures were concealed by a coquettish arrangement of lace, was of a gleaming white. Her hair was dressed almost like Madame du Barry's; her face, although overshadowed by a large cap, seemed only the daintier therefor, and the powder was very becoming to her. She smiled graciously at the sculptor. Sarrasine, disgusted beyond measure at finding himself unable to speak to her without witnesses, courteously seated himself beside her, and discoursed of music, extolling her prodigious talent; but his voice trembled with love and fear and hope.

"'What do you fear?' queried Vitagliani, the most celebrated singer in the troupe. 'Go on, you have no rival here to fear.'

"After he had said this the tenor smiled silently. The lips of all the guests repeated that smile, in which there was a lurking expression of malice likely to escape a lover. The publicity of his love was like a sudden dagger-thrust in Sarrasine's heart. Although possessed of a certain strength of character, and although nothing that might happen could subdue the violence of his passion, it had not before occurred to him that La Zambinella was almost a courtesan, and that he could not hope to enjoy at one and the same time the pure delights which would make a maiden's love so sweet, and the passionate transports with which one must purchase the perilous favors of an actress.

19

He reflected and resigned himself to his fate. The supper was served. Sarrasine and La Zambinella seated themselves side by side without ceremony. During the first half of the feast the artists exercised some restraint, and the sculptor was able to converse with the singer. He found that she was very bright and quick-witted; but she was amazingly ignorant and seemed weak and superstitious. The delicacy of her organs was reproduced in her understanding. When Vitagliani opened the first bottle of champagne, Sarrasine read in his neighbor's eyes a shrinking dread of the report caused by the release of the gas. The involuntary shudder of that thoroughly feminine temperament was interpreted by the amorous artist as indicating extreme delicacy of feeling. This weakness delighted the Frenchman. There is so much of the element of protection in a man's love!

"'You may make use of my power as a shield!'

"Is not that sentence written at the root of all declarations of love? Sarrasine, who was too passionately in love to make fine speeches to the fair Italian, was, like all lovers, grave, jovial, meditative, by turns. Although he seemed to listen to the guests, he did not hear a word that they said, he was so wrapped up in the pleasure of sitting by her side, of touching her hand, of waiting on her. He was swimming in a sea of concealed joy. Despite the eloquence of divers glances they exchanged, he was amazed at La Zambinella's continued reserve toward him. She had begun, it is true, by touching his foot with hers and stimulating his passion with the mischievous pleasure of a woman who is free and in love; but she had suddenly enveloped herself in maidenly modesty, after she had heard Sarrasine relate an incident which illustrated the extreme violence of his temper. When the supper became a debauch, the guests began to sing, inspired by the Peralta and the Pedro-Ximenes. There were fascinating duets, Calabrian ballads, Spanish *sequidillas*, and Neapolitan *canzonettes*. Drunkenness was in all eyes, in the music, in the hearts and voices of the guests. There was a sudden overflow of bewitching vivacity, of cordial unconstraint, of Italian good nature, of which no words can convey an idea to those who know only the evening parties of Paris, the routs of London, or the clubs of Vienna. Jests and words of love flew from side to side like bullets in a battle, amid laughter, impieties, invocations to the Blessed Virgin or the *Bambino*. One man lay on a sofa and fell asleep. A young woman listened to a declaration, unconscious that she was spilling Xeres wine on the tablecloth. Amid all this confusion La Zambinella, as if terror-stricken, seemed lost in thought. She refused to drink, but ate perhaps a little too much; but gluttony is attractive in women, it is said. Sarrasine, admiring his mistress' modesty, indulged in serious reflections concerning the future.

"'She desires to be married, I presume,' he said to himself.

"Thereupon he abandoned himself to blissful anticipations of marriage with her. It seemed to him that his whole life would be too short to exhaust the living spring of happiness which he found in the depths of his heart. Vitagliani, who sat on his other side, filled his glass so often that, about three in the morning, Sarrasine, while not absolutely drunk, was powerless to resist his delirious passion. In a moment of frenzy he seized the woman and carried her to a sort of boudoir which opened from the salon, and toward which he had more than once turned his eyes. The Italian was armed with a dagger.

"'If you come hear me,' she said, 'I shall be compelled to plunge this blade into your heart. Go! you would despise me. I have conceived too great a respect for your character to abandon myself to you thus. I do not choose to destroy the sentiment with which you honor me.'

"'Ah!' said Sarrasine, 'to stimulate a passion is a poor way to extinguish it! Are you already so corrupt that, being old in heart, you act like a young prostitute who inflames the emotions in which she trades?'

"'Why, this is Friday,' she replied, alarmed by the Frenchman's violence.

"Sarrasine, who was not piously inclined, began to laugh. La Zambinella gave a bound like a young deer, and darted into the salon. When Sarrasine appeared, running after her, he was welcomed by a roar of infernal laughter. He saw La Zambinella swooning on a sofa. She was very pale, as if exhausted by the extraordinary effort she had made. Although Sarrasine knew but little Italian, he understood his mistress when she said to Vitagliani in a low voice:

"'But he will kill me!'

"This strange scene abashed the sculptor. His reason returned. He stood still for a moment; then he recovered his speech, sat down beside his mistress, and assured her of his profound respect. He found strength to hold his passion in check while talking to her in the most exalted strain; and, to describe his love, he displayed all the treasures of eloquence—that sorcerer, that friendly interpreter, whom women rarely refuse to believe. When the first rays of dawn surprised the boon companions, some woman suggested that they go to Frascati. One and all welcomed with loud applause the idea of passing the day at Villa Ludovisi. Vitagliani went down to hire carriages. Sarrasine had the good fortune to drive La Zambinella in a phaeton. When they had left Rome behind, the merriment of the party, repressed for a moment by the battle they had all been fighting against drowsiness, suddenly awoke. All, men and women alike, seemed accustomed to that strange life, that constant round of pleasures, that artistic energy, which makes of life one never ending *fete*, where laughter reigns, unchecked by fear of the future. The sculptor's companion was the only one who seemed out of spirits.

"'Are you ill?' Sarrasine asked her. 'Would you prefer to go home?'

"'I am not strong enough to stand all this dissipation,' she replied. 'I have to be very careful; but I feel so happy with you! Except for you, I should not have remained to this supper; a night like this takes away all my freshness.'

"'You are so delicate!' rejoined Sarrasine, gazing in rapture at the charming creature's dainty features.

"'Dissipation ruins my voice.'

"'Now that we are alone,' cried the artist, 'and that you no longer have reason to fear the effervescence of my passion, tell me that you love me.'

"'Why?' said she; 'for what good purpose? You think me pretty. But you are a Frenchman, and your fancy will pass away. Ah! you would not love me as I should like to be loved.'

"'How?'

"'Purely, with no mingling of vulgar passion. I abhor men even more, perhaps than I hate women. I need to take refuge in friendship. The world is a desert to me. I am an accursed creature, doomed to understand happiness, to feel it, to desire it, and like many, many others, compelled to see it always fly from me. Remember, signor, that I have not deceived you. I forbid you to love me. I can be a devoted friend to you, for I admire your strength of will and your character. I need a brother, a protector. Be both of these to me, but nothing more.'

"'And not love you!' cried Sarrasine; 'but you are my life, my happiness, dear angel!'

"'If I should say a word, you would spurn me with horror.'

"'Coquette! nothing can frighten me. Tell me that you will cost me my whole future, that I shall die two months hence, that I shall be damned for having kissed you but once—'

"And he kissed her, despite La Zambinella's efforts to avoid that passionate caress.

"'Tell me that you are a demon, that I must give you my fortune, my name, all my renown! Would you have me cease to be a sculptor? Speak.'

"'Suppose I were not a woman?' queried La Zambinella, timidly, in a sweet, silvery voice.

"'A merry jest!' cried Sarrasine. 'Think you that you can deceive an artist's eye? Have I not, for ten days past, admired, examined, devoured, thy perfections? None but a woman can have this soft and beautifully rounded arm, these graceful outlines. Ah! you seek compliments!'

"She smiled sadly, and murmured:

"'Fatal beauty!'

"She raised her eyes to the sky. At that moment, there was in her eyes an indefinable expression of horror, so startling, so intense, that Sarrasine shuddered.

"'Signor Frenchman,' she continued, 'forget forever a moment's madness. I esteem you, but as for love, do not ask me for that; that sentiment is suffocated in my heart. I have no heart!' she cried, weeping bitterly. 'The stage on which you saw me, the applause, the music, the renown to which I am condemned—those are my life; I have no other. A few hours hence you will no longer look upon me with the same eyes, the woman you love will be dead.'

"The sculptor did not reply. He was seized with a dull rage which contracted his heart. He could do nothing but gaze at that extraordinary woman, with inflamed, burning eyes. That feeble voice, La Zambinella's attitude, manners, and gestures, instinct with dejection, melancholy, and discouragement, reawakened in his soul all the treasures of passion. Each word was a spur. At that moment, they arrived at Frascati. When the artist held out his arms to help his mistress to alight, he felt that she trembled from head to foot.

"'What is the matter? You would kill me,' he cried, seeing that she turned pale, 'if you should suffer the slightest pain of which I am, even innocently, the cause.'

"'A snake!' she said, pointing to a reptile which was gliding along the edge of a ditch. 'I am afraid of the disgusting creatures.'

"Sarrasine crushed the snake's head with a blow of his foot.

"'How could you dare to do it?' said La Zambinella, gazing at the dead reptile with visible terror.

"'Aha!' said the artist, with a smile, 'would you venture to say now that you are not a woman?'

"They joined their companions and walked through the woods of Villa Ludovisi, which at that time belonged to Cardinal Cicognara. The morning passed all too swiftly for the amorous sculptor, but it was crowded with incidents which laid bare to him the coquetry, the weakness, the daintiness, of that pliant, inert soul. She was a true woman with her sudden terrors, her unreasoning caprices, her instinctive worries, her causeless audacity, her bravado, and her fascinating delicacy of feeling. At one time, as the merry little party of singers ventured out into the open country, they saw at some distance a number of men armed to the teeth, whose costume was by no means reassuring. At the words, 'Those are brigands!' they all quickened their pace in order to reach the shelter of the wall enclosing the cardinal's villa. At that critical moment Sarrasine saw from La Zambinella's manner that she no longer had strength to walk; he took her in his arms and carried her for some distance, running. When he was within call of a vineyard near by, he set his mistress down.

"'Tell me,' he said, 'why it is that this extreme weakness which in another woman would be hideous, would disgust me, so that the slightest indication of it would be enough to destroy my love,—why is it that in you it pleases me, fascinates me? Oh, how I love you!' he continued. 'All your faults, your frights, your petty foibles, add an indescribable charm to your character. I feel that I should detest a Sappho, a strong, courageous woman, overflowing with energy and passion. O sweet and fragile creature! how couldst thou be otherwise? That angel's voice, that refined voice, would have been an anachronism coming from any other breast than thine.'

"'I can give you no hope,' she said. 'Cease to speak thus to me, for people would make sport of you. It is impossible for me to shut the door of the theatre to you; but if you love me, or if you are wise, you will come there no more. Listen to me, monsieur,' she continued in a grave voice.

"'Oh, hush!' said the excited artist. 'Obstacles inflame the love in my heart.'

"La Zambinella maintained a graceful and modest attitude; but she held her peace, as if a terrible thought had suddenly revealed some catastrophe. When it was time to return to Rome she entered a berlin with four seats, bidding the sculptor, with a cruelly imperious air, to return alone in the phaeton. On the road, Sarrasine determined to carry off La Zambinella. He passed the whole day forming plans, each more extravagant than the last. At nightfall, as he was going out to inquire of somebody where his mistress lived, he met one of his fellow-artists at the door.

"'My dear fellow,' he said, I am sent by our ambassador to invite you to come to the embassy this evening. He gives a magnificent concert, and when I tell you that La Zambinella will be there—'

"'Zambinella!' cried Sarrasine, thrown into delirium by that name; 'I am mad with love of her.'

"'You are like everybody else,' replied his comrade.

"'But if you are friends of mine, you and Vien and Lauterbourg and Allegrain, you will lend me your assistance for a *coup de main*, after the entertainment, will you not?' asked Sarrasine.

"'There's no cardinal to be killed? no—?'

"'No, no!' said Sarrasine, 'I ask nothing of you that men of honor may not do.'

"In a few moments the sculptor laid all his plans to assure the success of his enterprise. He was one of the last to arrive at the ambassador's, but he went thither in a traveling carriage drawn by four stout horses and driven by one of the most skilful *vetturini* in

Rome. The ambassador's palace was full of people; not without difficulty did the sculptor, whom nobody knew, make his way to the salon where La Zambinella was singing at that moment.

"'It must be in deference to all the cardinals, bishops, and *abbes* who are here,' said Sarrasine, 'that *she* is dressed as a man, that *she* has curly hair which *she* wears in a bag, and that *she* has a sword at her side?'

"'She! what she?' rejoined the old nobleman whom Sarrasine addressed.

"'La Zambinella.'

"'La Zambinella!' echoed the Roman prince. 'Are you jesting? Whence have you come? Did a woman ever appear in a Roman theatre? And do you not know what sort of creatures play female parts within the domains of the Pope? It was I, monsieur, who endowed Zambinella with his voice. I paid all the knave's expenses, even his teacher in singing. And he has so little gratitude for the service I have done him that he has never been willing to step inside my house. And yet, if he makes his fortune, he will owe it all to me.'

"Prince Chigi might have talked on forever, Sarrasine did not listen to him. A ghastly truth had found its way into his mind. He was stricken as if by a thunderbolt. He stood like a statue, his eyes fastened on the singer. His flaming glance exerted a sort of magnetic influence on Zambinella, for he turned his eyes at last in Sarrasine's direction, and his divine voice faltered. He trembled! An involuntary murmur escaped the audience, which he held fast as if fastened to his lips; and that completely disconcerted him; he stopped in the middle of the aria he was singing and sat down. Cardinal Cicognara, who had watched from the corner of his eye the direction of his *protege's* glance, saw the Frenchman; he leaned toward one of his ecclesiastical aides-de-camp, and apparently asked the sculptor's name. When he had obtained the reply he desired he scrutinized the artist with great attention and gave orders to an *abbe*, who instantly disappeared. Meanwhile Zambinella, having recovered his self-possession, resumed the aria he had so capriciously broken off; but he sang badly, and refused, despite all the persistent appeals showered upon him, to sing anything else. It was the first time he had exhibited that humorsome tyranny, which, at a later date, contributed no less to his celebrity than his talent and his vast fortune, which was said to be due to his beauty as much as to his voice.

"'It's a woman,' said Sarrasine, thinking that no one could overhear him. 'There's some secret intrigue beneath all this. Cardinal Cicognara is hoodwinking the Pope and the whole city of Rome!'

"The sculptor at once left the salon, assembled his friends, and lay in wait in the courtyard of the palace. When Zambinella was assured of Sarrasine's departure he seemed to recover his tranquillity in some measure. About midnight after wandering through the salons like a man looking for an enemy, the *musico* left the party. As he passed through the palace gate he was seized by men who deftly gagged him with a handkerchief and placed him in the carriage hired by Sarrasine. Frozen with terror, Zambinella lay back in a corner, not daring to move a muscle. He saw before him the terrible face of the artist, who maintained a deathlike silence. The journey was a short one. Zambinella, kidnaped by Sarrasine, soon found himself in a dark, bare studio. He sat, half dead, upon a chair, hardly daring to glance at a statue of a woman, in which he recognized his own features. He did not utter a word, but his teeth were chattering; he was paralyzed with fear. Sarrasine was striding up and down the studio. Suddenly he halted in front of Zambinella.

"'Tell me the truth,' he said, in a changed and hollow voice. 'Are you not a woman? Cardinal Cicognara—'

"Zambinella fell on his knees, and replied only by hanging his head.

"'Ah! you are a woman!' cried the artist in a frenzy; 'for even a—'

"He did not finish the sentence.

"'No,' he continued, 'even *he* could not be so utterly base.'

"'Oh, do not kill me!' cried Zambinella, bursting into tears. 'I consented to deceive you only to gratify my comrades, who wanted an opportunity to laugh.'

"'Laugh!' echoed the sculptor, in a voice in which there was a ring of infernal ferocity. 'Laugh! laugh! You dared to make sport of a man's passion—you?'

"'Oh, mercy!' cried Zambinella.

"'I ought to kill you!' shouted Sarrasine, drawing his sword in an outburst of rage. 'But,' he continued, with cold disdain, 'if I searched your whole being with this blade, should I find there any sentiment to blot out, anything with which to satisfy my thirst for vengeance? You are nothing! If you were a man or a woman, I would kill you, but—'

"Sarrasine made a gesture of disgust, and turned his face away; thereupon he noticed the statue.

"'And that is a delusion!' he cried.

"Then, turning to Zambinella once more, he continued:

"'A woman's heart was to me a place of refuge, a fatherland. Have you sisters who resemble you? No. Then die! But no, you shall live. To leave you your life is to doom you to a fate worse than death. I regret neither my blood nor my life, but my future and the fortune of my heart. Your weak hand has overturned my happiness. What hope can I extort from you in place of all those you have destroyed? You have brought me down to your level. *To love, to be loved!* are henceforth meaningless words to me, as to you. I shall never cease to think of that imaginary woman when I see a real woman.'

"He pointed to the statue with a gesture of despair.

"'I shall always have in my memory a divine harpy who will bury her talons in all my manly sentiments, and who will stamp all other women with a seal of imperfection. Monster! you, who can give life to nothing, have swept all women off the face of the earth.'

"Sarrasine seated himself in front of the terrified singer. Two great tears came from his dry eyes, rolled down his swarthy cheeks, and fell to the floor—two tears of rage, two scalding, burning tears.

"'An end of love! I am dead to all pleasure, to all human emotions!'

"As he spoke, he seized a hammer and hurled it at the statue with such excessive force that he missed it. He thought that he had destroyed that monument of his madness, and thereupon he drew his sword again, and raised it to kill the singer. Zambinella uttered shriek after shriek. Three men burst into the studio at that moment, and the sculptor fell, pieced by three daggers.

"'From Cardinal Cicognara,' said one of the men.

"'A benefaction worthy of a Christian,' retorted the Frenchman, as he breathed his last.

"These ominous emissaries told Zambinella of the anxiety of his patron, who was waiting at the door in a closed carriage in order to take him away as soon as he was set at liberty."

"But," said Madame de Rochefide, "what connection is there between this story and the little old man we saw at the Lantys'?"

"Madame, Cardinal Cicognara took possession of Zambinella's statue and had it reproduced in marble; it is in the Albani Museum to-day. In 1794 the Lanty family discovered it there, and asked Vien to copy it. The portrait which showed you Zambinella at twenty, a moment after you had seen him as a centenarian, afterward figured in Girodet's *Endymion*; you yourself recognized the type in *Adonis*."

"But this Zambinella, male or female—"

"Must be, madame, Marianina's maternal great uncle. You can conceive now Madame de Lanty's interest in concealing the source of a fortune which comes—"

"Enough!" said she, with an imperious gesture.

We remained for a moment in the most profound silence.

"Well?" I said at last.

"Ah!" she cried, rising and pacing the floor.

She came and looked me in the face, and said in an altered voice:

"You have disgusted me with life and passion for a long time to come. Leaving monstrosities aside, are not all human sentiments dissolved thus, by ghastly disillusionment? Children torture mothers by their bad conduct, or their lack of affection. Wives are betrayed. Mistresses are cast aside, abandoned. Talk of friendship! Is there such a thing! I would turn pious to-morrow if I did not know that I can remain like the inaccessible summit of a cliff amid the tempests of life. If the future of the Christian is an illusion too, at all events it is not destroyed until after death. Leave me to myself."

"Ah!" said I, "you know how to punish."

"Am I in the wrong?"

"Yes," I replied, with a sort of desperate courage. "By finishing this story, which is well known in Italy, I can give you an excellent idea of the progress made by the civilization of the present day. There are none of those wretched creatures now."

"Paris," said she, "is an exceedingly hospitable place; it welcomes one and all, fortunes stained with shame, and fortunes stained with blood. Crime and infamy have a right of asylum here; virtue alone is without altars. But pure hearts have a fatherland in heaven! No one will have known me! I am proud of it."

And the marchioness was lost in thought.